JOHNNY REB

Alan Archambault

Cover by Donna Neary

of John Knill as the charging bugle boy

Southern Militia

The American South has a long, proud, military tradition that dates back to the colonial days. In the years prior to the War Between the States a number of elite militia units existed throughout the South. Many of these units were composed of the finest young gentlemen of the community and were often dressed in elegant military uniforms. When the South went to war these militia units proudly joined the Confederate ranks where their training and enthusiasm provided a nucleus for the new Confederate army.

Company Officer, Clinch Rifles of Augusta, Georgia: Green uniform with gold trim, yellow pompon, and red sash. He carries an early Confederate national colors.

Private, Charleston Zouaves of South Carolina: Gray uniform with red cap, collar, cuffs, epaulets, and trouser stripe. White belts.

Private, Richmond Grays of Virginia: Gray uniform with black trim. White belts, plume, and epaulet fringe.

Private, Washington Light Infantry of Charleston, SC: Dark blue uniform with gold trim. Red leather belt. Red pompon and trouser stripe.

Johnny Reb's Farewell

In the spring of 1861, thousands of Confederate volunteers left their homes and loved ones to defend the rights and honor of the South. Ahead of them was a bloody and bitter war in which many would suffer and fall for the "lost cause."

1st Special Battalion, Louisiana Infantry (Wheat's Tigers), 1861-1862

Major Roberdeau Chatham Wheat recruited his colorful unit primarily from Irish roustabouts found on the wharfs of New Orleans. The unit's troops soon became notorious for their unruly behavior. However, in battle they lived up to their nickname of "Tigers." The Tigers were one of two Confederate units to adopt uniforms based on those made popular by French Algerian units who fought with distinction in the Crimean War. Their uniforms consisted of blue jackets with red trim, red shirts and sashes, and full trousers made of a blue and white striped material. Headgear was either a red fez with blue tassel or a slouch hat. The hats often had bands emblazoned with mottoes and slogans like "Tiger by Nature," or "Lincoln's Life or a Tiger's Death." After Wheat was killed at Gaines's Mill in June 1862 the Battalion was disbanded and its men assigned to other Louisiana regiments.

The Confederate Infantry

The foot soldiers who wore the gray (or butternut) created a legacy of service unmatched in American history. The Rebel infantry proved aggressive on the attack and stubborn on defense. Generally, the Southern soldier had great trust in his military leaders and this faith, coupled with aggressive, superior, leadership, proved an effective combination. In spite of limited manpower and material resources the Confederate infantryman fought bravely for four years, winning the respect and admiration of his Northern foe.

Confederate Infantryman—Army of Northern Virginia

This rugged foot soldier represents a typical soldier of the Army of Northern Virginia as he may have appeared from 1862 to 1865. His jacket and belt plate are of the style issued primarily to Confederate forces in the eastern theater while his slouch hat and Enfield rifled musket are typical of all Southern infantry. He carries extra clothing rolled in his blanket and tucks the cuffs of his trousers into his socks. He reaches into his cartridge box to get a cartridge for his weapon.

Clothing

1. Confederate infantryman wearing a handsewn shirt and drawers made of cotton sheeting. Drawers have drawstring closures on cuffs. 2. Typical slouch hat favored by Confederate troops. This example features a beehive-style crown. 3. Suspenders (braces) for holding up trousers. 4. Trousers made of gray wool cloth. 5. Leather brogans (shoes). Keeping the Confederate soldier shod in good footwear was always a problem for the army. 6. Confederate issue cotton socks. 7. Rear view of Confederate jacket illustrating belt loops and seams. 8. Infantry jacket of the type issued to Eastern troops circa 1862-1864 and worn to the end of the war. It is made of gray wool with blue edging on the shoulder straps. 9. Brass infantry jacket buttons.

Confederate Infantryman's Equipment

In spite of the limited manufacturing resources of the Southern states, the Confederate government did a good job of supplying Johnny Reb with the basic accoutrements needed to wage war. 1. Waistbelt with C.S.A. belt plate. 2. Cap box with flap open. 3. Cartridge box. 4. Waistbelt with forked tongue buckle. 5. Waistbelt with oval C.S. plate. 6. Bayonet scabbard. 7. Tin-drum-style canteen. 8. Wood canteen. 9. Cloth ditty bag. 10. Tin drinking cup. 11. Canvas haversack. 12. Blanket roll. 13. Combination folding knife and spoon. 14. Sewing kit. 15. Soldier's wallet. 16. Confederate knapsack.

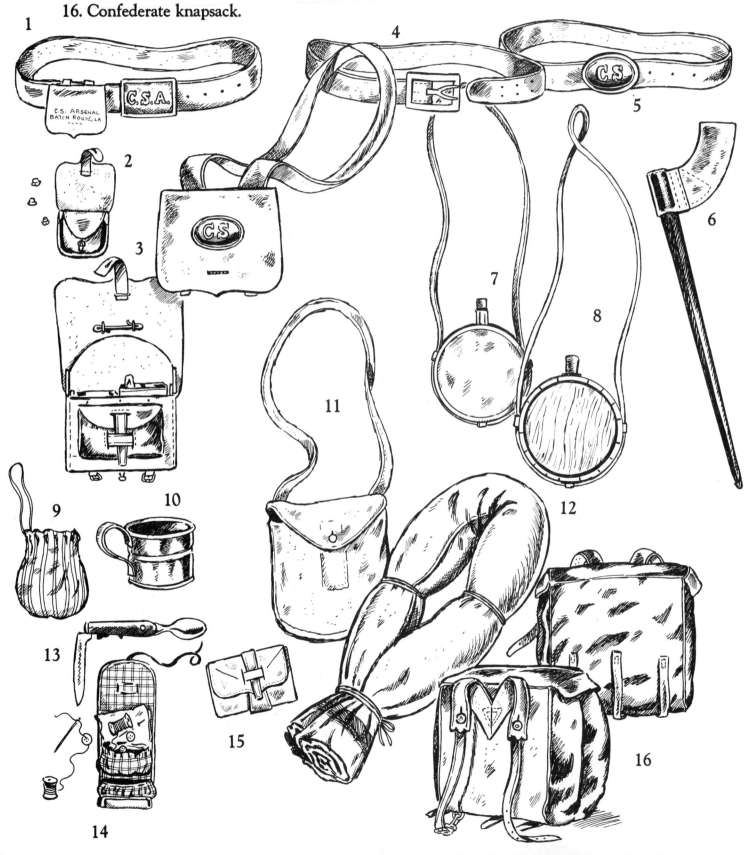

Infantry Muskets and Rifles

The Confederate infantryman used a variety of long arms during the course of the Civil War. A number of Federal weapons were in the hands of Southern militia units and stored in Southern armories at the beginning of the war. Of course, these were confiscated for use by the Confederate forces. Other U.S. weapons were captured in battle or in raids of Northern supply trains. The Confederacy also purchased many weapons in Europe. The most popular of these foreign weapons was the British Enfield rifle musket. The Confederates also manufactured their own firearms. Armories were established in Richmond, Virginia and Fayetteville, North Carolina. Using arms-producing machinery captured from the U.S. Arsenal at Harper's Ferry, the Confederates produced over 64,000 rifles and rifle muskets at their armories. A number of Southern gunsmiths also produced a wide array of firearms under contract to the Confederate, or state governments.

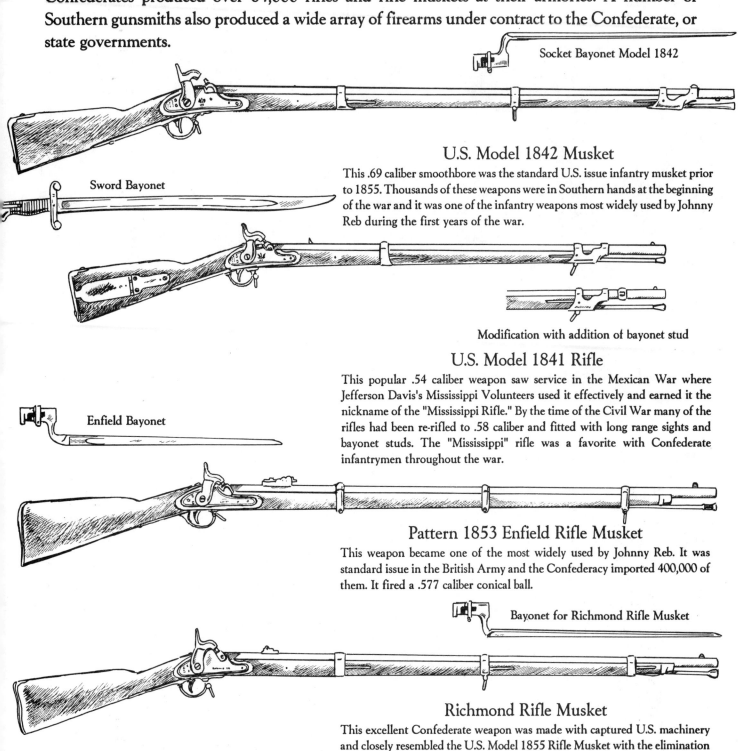

Socket Bayonet Model 1842

U.S. Model 1842 Musket

This .69 caliber smoothbore was the standard U.S. issue infantry musket prior to 1855. Thousands of these weapons were in Southern hands at the beginning of the war and it was one of the infantry weapons most widely used by Johnny Reb during the first years of the war.

Sword Bayonet

Modification with addition of bayonet stud

U.S. Model 1841 Rifle

This popular .54 caliber weapon saw service in the Mexican War where Jefferson Davis's Mississippi Volunteers used it effectively and earned it the nickname of the "Mississippi Rifle." By the time of the Civil War many of the rifles had been re-rifled to .58 caliber and fitted with long range sights and bayonet studs. The "Mississippi" rifle was a favorite with Confederate infantrymen throughout the war.

Enfield Bayonet

Pattern 1853 Enfield Rifle Musket

This weapon became one of the most widely used by Johnny Reb. It was standard issue in the British Army and the Confederacy imported 400,000 of them. It fired a .577 caliber conical ball.

Bayonet for Richmond Rifle Musket

Richmond Rifle Musket

This excellent Confederate weapon was made with captured U.S. machinery and closely resembled the U.S. Model 1855 Rifle Musket with the elimination of the tape primer system. It fired a .58 caliber minié ball.

Loading a Civil War Rifle Musket

The standard weapon of the Confederate Infantryman was a muzzle-loading, .58 Caliber rifle musket. It fired a soft lead "minié" bullet which was accurate up to 500 yards. Cartridges containing powder and bullet were wrapped in paper and carried in a cartridge box. In spite of the laborious loading procedure, a well trained soldier could load and fire three shots per minute. The Confederate soldier illustrated here is armed with a Richmond made copy of a U.S. Model 1855 rifle musket.

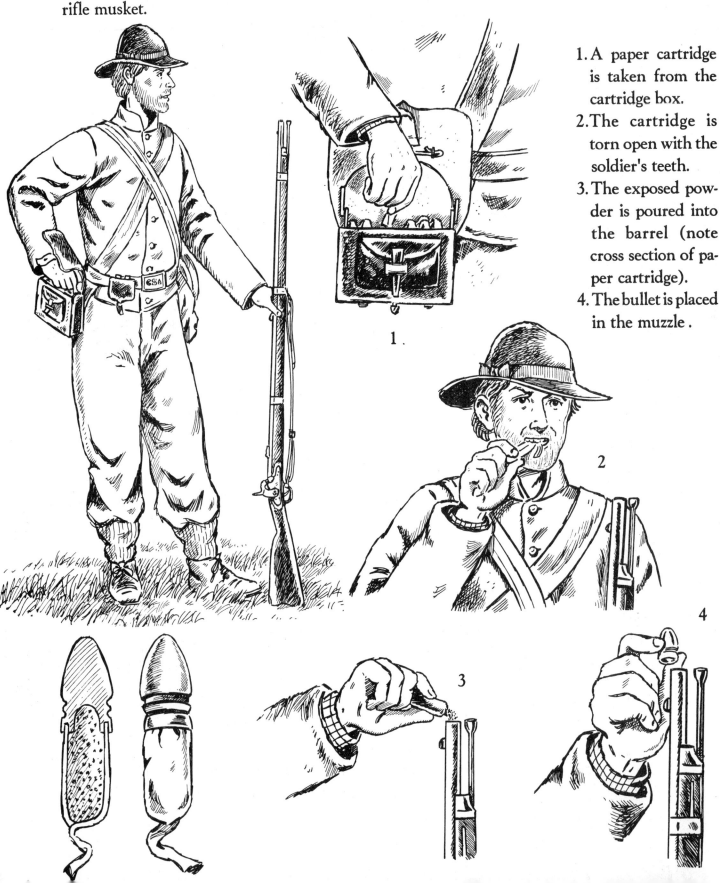

1. A paper cartridge is taken from the cartridge box.
2. The cartridge is torn open with the soldier's teeth.
3. The exposed powder is poured into the barrel (note cross section of paper cartridge).
4. The bullet is placed in the muzzle.

5. The ramrod is taken from its position under the barrel and pushed down the barrel forcing the bullet and powder down to the bottom of the barrel.

6. A percussion cap is taken from the cap pouch.

7. The hammer is brought to half cock and a percussion cap is placed on the musket nipple.

8. The hammer may now be brought to full cock and the weapon is ready to fire.

Confederate Flags

National flag of the Confederate States of America, the "Stars and Bars." Blue canton with white stars and red, white, and red bars. The eleven stars represent the Confederate States of July to November 1861.

First flag of the Confederate States of America with seven white stars in a blue canton with red, white, and red bars. Adopted on March 4, 1861.

"The bonnie blue flag that bears the single star." Blue field with white star. January, 1861.

Flag of the Confederate States of America, May 1, 1863 - March 4, 1865, the "Stainless Banner."

Confederate Navy Jack, May 26, 1863.

Confederate Navy Jack, March 4, 1861 - May 26, 1863. Blue field with white stars.

Red field with blue "Southern Cross" with white border and stars.

Flag of the Confederate States of America. Adopted on March 4, 1865. This version featured the red stripe.

Battle Flags

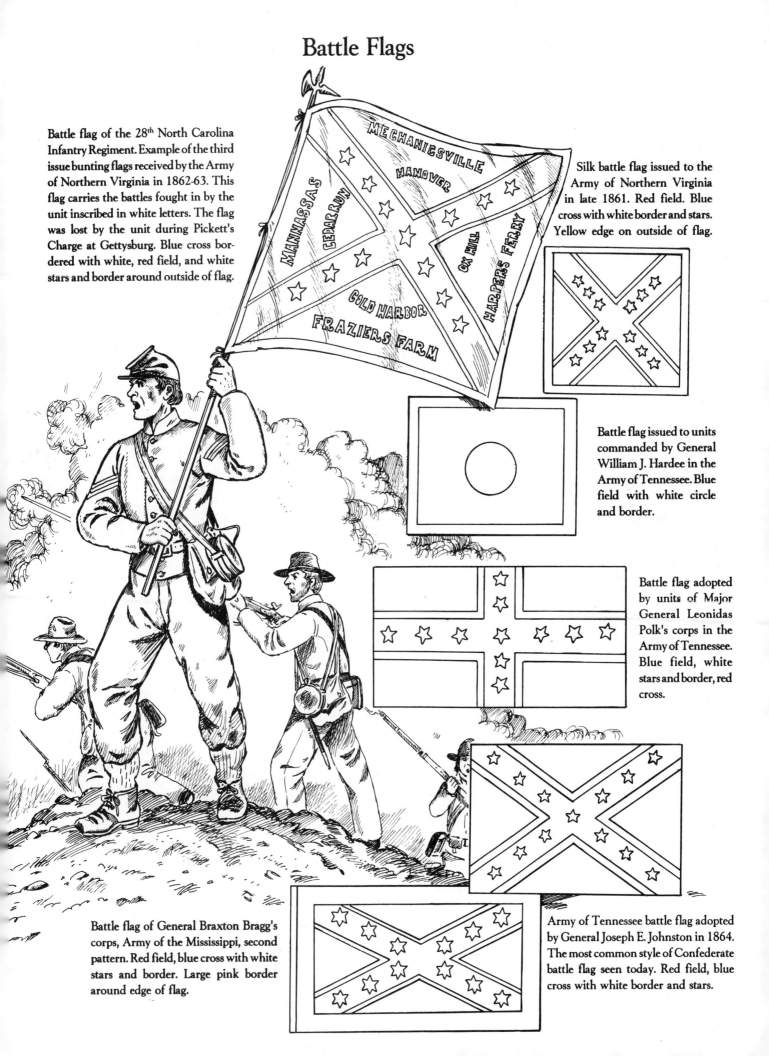

Battle flag of the 28th North Carolina Infantry Regiment. Example of the third issue bunting flags received by the Army of Northern Virginia in 1862-63. This flag carries the battles fought in by the unit inscribed in white letters. The flag was lost by the unit during Pickett's Charge at Gettysburg. Blue cross bordered with white, red field, and white stars and border around outside of flag.

Silk battle flag issued to the Army of Northern Virginia in late 1861. Red field. Blue cross with white border and stars. Yellow edge on outside of flag.

Battle flag issued to units commanded by General William J. Hardee in the Army of Tennessee. Blue field with white circle and border.

Battle flag adopted by units of Major General Leonidas Polk's corps in the Army of Tennessee. Blue field, white stars and border, red cross.

Battle flag of General Braxton Bragg's corps, Army of the Mississippi, second pattern. Red field, blue cross with white stars and border. Large pink border around edge of flag.

Army of Tennessee battle flag adopted by General Joseph E. Johnston in 1864. The most common style of Confederate battle flag seen today. Red field, blue cross with white border and stars.

Johnny Reb's Heroes

From the very beginning of the Civil War the Southern forces were blessed with outstanding generals, especially in the eastern theater. Talented Confederate generals like "Stonewall" Jackson, J.E.B. Stuart, and Robert E. Lee soon earned the respect, confidence and love of the soldiers in the ranks. Indeed, General Lee, nicknamed "Marse Robert" by the troops, was revered by the men of his Army of Northern Virginia. Whenever his men saw him they excitedly cheered their beloved leader. The faith and confidence the Confederate soldiers had in their able leaders helped sustain them in their heroic struggle against the larger and better equipped Union army.

Southern Women

The women of the South were responsible, in great measure, for holding the Confederacy together while most of the men were at the front. Toiling in fields and factories, they supplied the men with food, clothing, equipment and munitions. Some women served as spies and scouts and many others as nurses, giving aid and comfort to the sick and wounded. The sacrifice and courage of the Southern women certainly matched the bravery of the men in gray.

For more about these brave women you will want *Heroines of the Civil War*; see inside back cover.

Confederate Headgear

1. Slouch hat worn by Confederate cavalry officer with the brim turned up and adorned with a plume. This "Cavalier" image was popular with dashing Rebel horsemen. 2. Enlisted man's kepi of gray wool with a blue band around base. 3. Pre-war style forage cap which continued to be worn by some Southern units during the early years of the war. 4. Gray "Sicilian" or "Phrygian" fatigue cap which saw some popularity among Southern volunteers. 5. White linen havelock worn over kepi. It was intended to ward off sunstroke. 6. Confederate officer's kepi featuring gold braid indicative of his rank. In this case two strands of braid signifies the rank of captain. 7. Soft brimmed slouch hat popular throughout the Confederate forces. It was practical and comfortable and was available in many styles and colors. 8. Common style of forage cap worn by Southern soldiers.

Fighting Knives

At the beginning of the Civil War no self-respecting Johnny Reb would be without a ferocious looking fighting knife. There were many styles of knives, but most were called "Bowie" knives, after James Bowie, the famous knife fighter who died at the Alamo. Blades of the fighting knives ranged from 8 to 20 inches and some featured D-shaped knuckle guards. In actual combat the knives seldom drew blood but were useful in camp for all types of chores from skinning game to cutting brush.

Confederate "Foot Cavalry"

As the war progressed, the tough, lean, Confederate infantry earned a reputation for their determined and rapid marches. During Thomas J. "Stonewall" Jackson's Shenandoah Valley Campaign, in 1862, the II Corps, Army of Northern Virginia marched 400 miles, fought five pitched battles, and defeated three Union commands in a period of only six weeks. Their spectacular performance earned them the nickname of "Jackson's Foot Cavalry."

In the summer of 1864, the II Corps, under Lt. Gen. Jubal Early, raided the North, marching over 500 rugged miles in five weeks. Their former commander, Jackson, who was killed in 1863, would have been proud of them.

Confederate Cavalry

In the opening days of the Civil War the Confederate cavalry had a natural edge over their Northern opponents. In many areas of the South life revolved around horses and horsemanship. Many young Southern volunteers had literally "grown up in the saddle" and were excellent material for Confederate cavalry units. Confederate recruits usually supplied their own horses so the early Confederate cavalry units were mounted on excellent horseflesh. In the first two years of the war the Confederate cavalry practically rode rings around the Union troopers. As the war progressed, however, Southern horses, manpower, and equipment were gradually depleted and the Union cavalry eventually became the equal to the horsemen in gray.

Officer

Trooper

Color Bearer

Confederate Cavalry Uniforms

The Confederate cavalry trooper was one of the most dashing soldiers of the war, as reflected in his varied and colorful dress. The trooper on the left wears a captured Union greatcoat and saber belt and is armed with a shotgun. To his left a trooper from the 1st Virginia Cavalry Regiment, "Black Horse Cavalry," wears a gray uniform with black slouch hat and plume. Next, a member of the Sussex Light Dragoons, Virginia State Cavalry, wears a gray battle shirt and tall blue forage cap. The kneeling trooper fires a single-shot Cook carbine made in Athens, Georgia. On the right a Confederate lieutenant wears a jacket with yellow cavalry trim. The flag is the one carried by the 1st Virginia Cavalry.

Confederate Cavalry Weapons

Confederate Cavalry troopers were armed with many types of weapons, from captured Yankee pistols to imported arms, to Southern manufactured carbines. A few of these weapons are shown here.

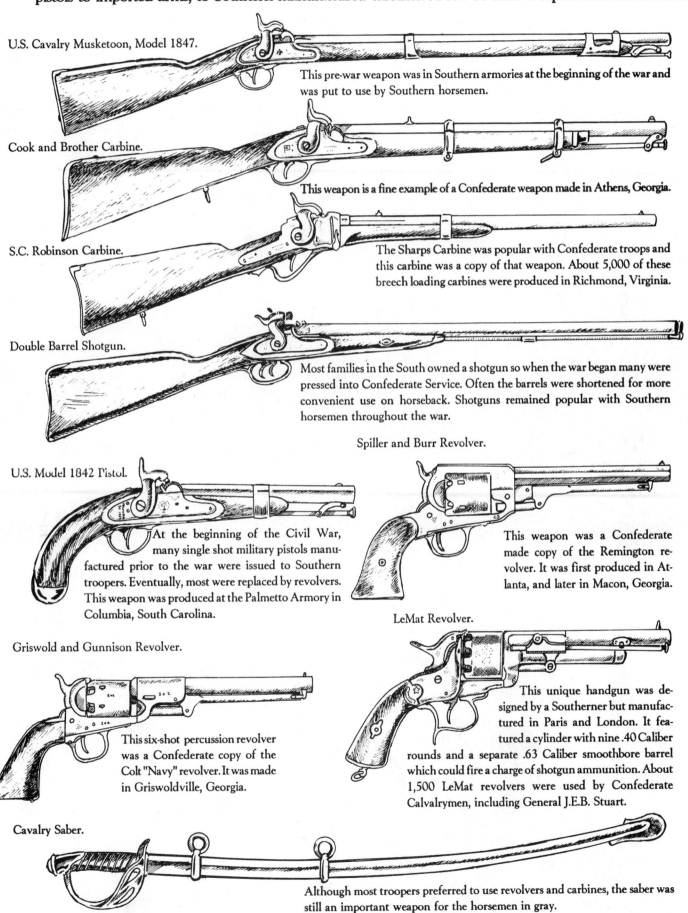

U.S. Cavalry Musketoon, Model 1847.

This pre-war weapon was in Southern armories at the beginning of the war and was put to use by Southern horsemen.

Cook and Brother Carbine.

This weapon is a fine example of a Confederate weapon made in Athens, Georgia.

S.C. Robinson Carbine.

The Sharps Carbine was popular with Confederate troops and this carbine was a copy of that weapon. About 5,000 of these breech loading carbines were produced in Richmond, Virginia.

Double Barrel Shotgun.

Most families in the South owned a shotgun so when the war began many were pressed into Confederate Service. Often the barrels were shortened for more convenient use on horseback. Shotguns remained popular with Southern horsemen throughout the war.

Spiller and Burr Revolver.

U.S. Model 1842 Pistol.

At the beginning of the Civil War, many single shot military pistols manufactured prior to the war were issued to Southern troopers. Eventually, most were replaced by revolvers. This weapon was produced at the Palmetto Armory in Columbia, South Carolina.

This weapon was a Confederate made copy of the Remington revolver. It was first produced in Atlanta, and later in Macon, Georgia.

LeMat Revolver.

Griswold and Gunnison Revolver.

This six-shot percussion revolver was a Confederate copy of the Colt "Navy" revolver. It was made in Griswoldville, Georgia.

This unique handgun was designed by a Southerner but manufactured in Paris and London. It featured a cylinder with nine .40 Caliber rounds and a separate .63 Caliber smoothbore barrel which could fire a charge of shotgun ammunition. About 1,500 LeMat revolvers were used by Confederate Calvalrymen, including General J.E.B. Stuart.

Cavalry Saber.

Although most troopers preferred to use revolvers and carbines, the saber was still an important weapon for the horsemen in gray.

The loading and firing of a muzzle-loading cannon was a procedure which took teamwork and precision. Each member of the crew had an assigned position and function. An experienced team could load and fire two aimed shot per minute. This illustration depicts a four-gun battery demonstrating the steps involved in the serving of the gun "by the numbers."

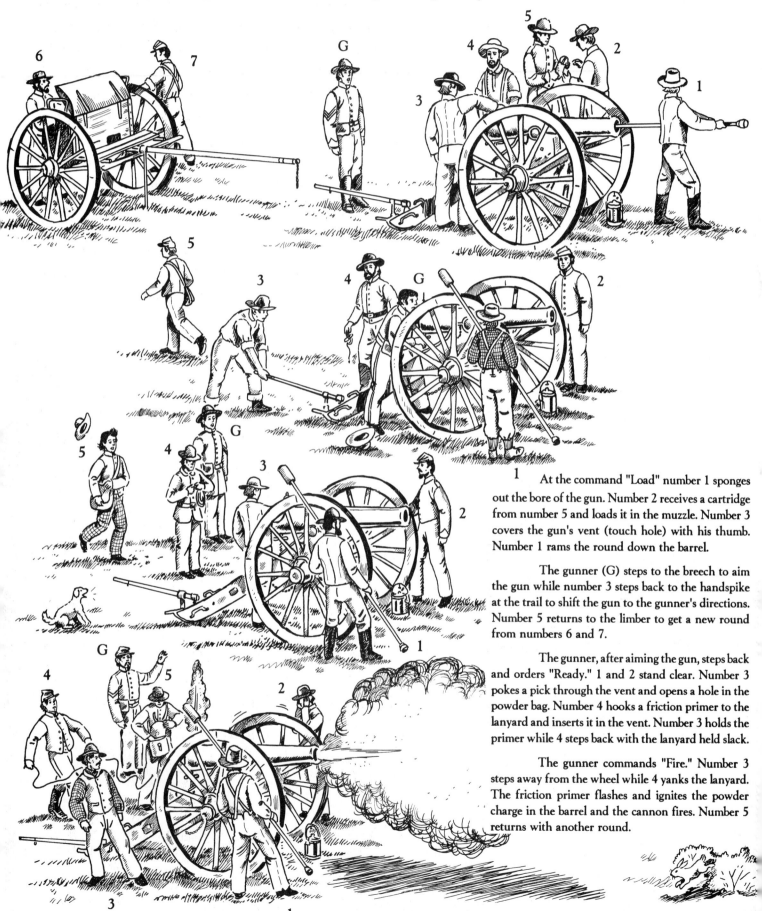

1   At the command "Load" number 1 sponges out the bore of the gun. Number 2 receives a cartridge from number 5 and loads it in the muzzle. Number 3 covers the gun's vent (touch hole) with his thumb. Number 1 rams the round down the barrel.

The gunner (G) steps to the breech to aim the gun while number 3 steps back to the handspike at the trail to shift the gun to the gunner's directions. Number 5 returns to the limber to get a new round from numbers 6 and 7.

The gunner, after aiming the gun, steps back and orders "Ready." 1 and 2 stand clear. Number 3 pokes a pick through the vent and opens a hole in the powder bag. Number 4 hooks a friction primer to the lanyard and inserts it in the vent. Number 3 holds the primer while 4 steps back with the lanyard held slack.

The gunner commands "Fire." Number 3 steps away from the wheel while 4 yanks the lanyard. The friction primer flashes and ignites the powder charge in the barrel and the cannon fires. Number 5 returns with another round.

Confederate Artillery

At the beginning of the Civil War, the Confederate forces were at a distinct disadvantage in the number of artillery pieces and trained artillerymen available for service in their army. A few cannon fell into Southern hands in the early days of the war, but the North had the advantages of an existing artillery corps and the foundries capable of producing quality pieces of artillery. In the first years of the war, the Confederates were outgunned by the gunners in blue and it was only through determination and courage that the Rebel artillerymen held their ground. Confederate foundries did an amazing job of producing excellent cannons with limited resources and gray cannoneers learned their trade on the battlefield. Several Confederate artillery units like the Richmond Howitzers and the Washington Artillery of New Orleans earned reputations for bravery and ability to rival any Union battery.

Field Guns

The Confederates used a variety of cannons during the war including older cannon in the hands of militia units, guns captured from the Federals, imported artillery, and guns made by Southern foundries. A sample of the many types are illustrated here.

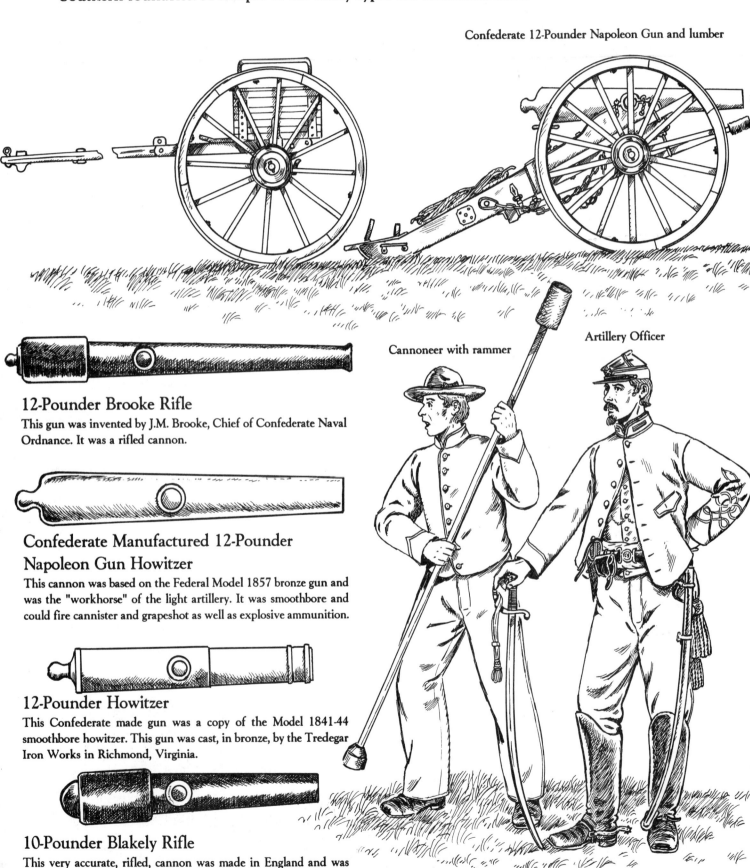

Confederate 12-Pounder Napoleon Gun and lumber

Cannoneer with rammer

Artillery Officer

12-Pounder Brooke Rifle

This gun was invented by J.M. Brooke, Chief of Confederate Naval Ordnance. It was a rifled cannon.

Confederate Manufactured 12-Pounder Napoleon Gun Howitzer

This cannon was based on the Federal Model 1857 bronze gun and was the "workhorse" of the light artillery. It was smoothbore and could fire cannister and grapeshot as well as explosive ammunition.

12-Pounder Howitzer

This Confederate made gun was a copy of the Model 1841-44 smoothbore howitzer. This gun was cast, in bronze, by the Tredegar Iron Works in Richmond, Virginia.

10-Pounder Blakely Rifle

This very accurate, rifled, cannon was made in England and was imported by the Confederacy in limited numbers.

Seacoast Artillery

The Confederacy had 3,000 miles of coastline to defend from Federal invaders and a number of forts were garrisoned at strategic ports on the coasts and waterways. Large cannons usually were mounted in these forts and they were manned by dedicated Confederate artillerymen. In spite of fierce Union attacks, some of these Confederate strongholds withstood terrible sieges until the last stages of the war.

24-Pounder Siege and Garrison Gun on a Casemate Carriage

32-Pounder Seacoast Gun on a Barbette Carriage

Confederate Artillerymen man Rodman Cannons at the siege of Fort Fisher, North Carolina

Mosby's Partisan Rangers

After serving with the First Virginia Cavalry and as a scout for General J.E.B. Stuart, John Singleton Mosby was given permission to form a band of irregular forces. Using the exploits of his hero Francis Marion, the "Swamp Fox" of the American Revolution, as inspiration, Mosby led his 43rd Battalion of Partisan Rangers on many remarkable adventures. His rangers raided Union supply trains, camps, and outposts and captured many prisoners including a general. The Yankees began to call Mosby the "Gray Ghost" and committed thousands of troops to his capture. Mosby continually evaded his Northern foes and his area of operations in Virginia became known as "Mosby's Confederacy."

Here one of Mosby's Rangers captures a Union Cavalryman. Ranger: Gray Uniform with buff gauntlets (gloves). Yankee: Dark blue jacket with yellow braid and light blue trousers.

Confederate Officers

Most of the Southern states had a strong, cherished, tradition of military service that provided the Confederate Army with a number of able and enthusiastic officers. Many experienced officers serving with the United States Army resigned when their home state seceded or when the conflict actually began. Over 300 actually resigned their United States commissions to serve the Confederacy. Existing militia units also provided the South with trained officers, while a number of eager young volunteer officers proved themselves on the field of battle. Throughout the war, dedicated officers in gray fought, and often died, for their beliefs in Southern rights.

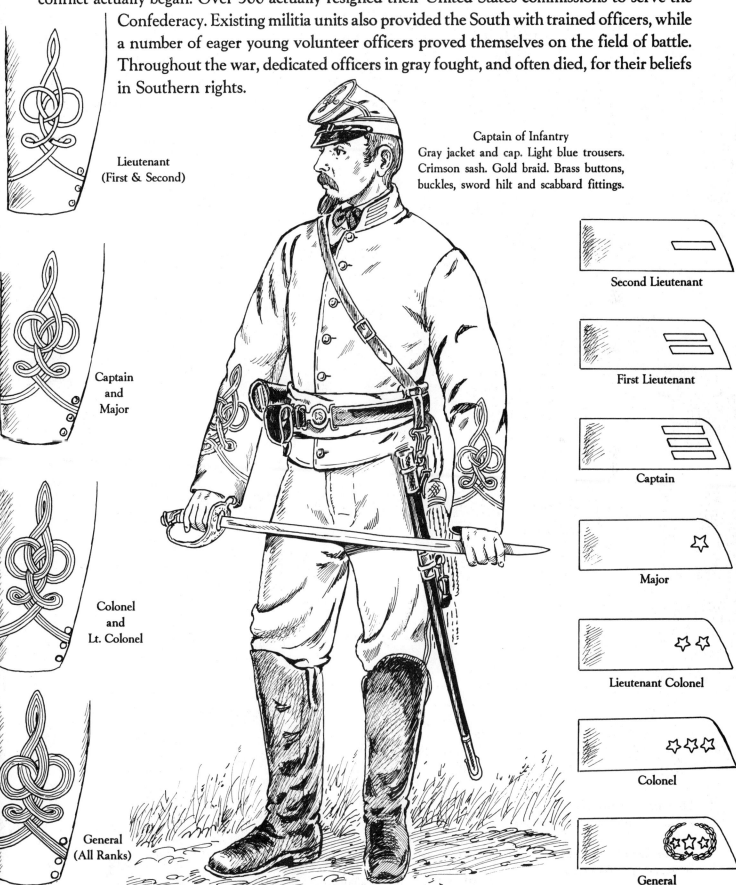

Lieutenant
(First & Second)

Captain
and
Major

Colonel
and
Lt. Colonel

General
(All Ranks)

Captain of Infantry
Gray jacket and cap. Light blue trousers. Crimson sash. Gold braid. Brass buttons, buckles, sword hilt and scabbard fittings.

Second Lieutenant

First Lieutenant

Captain

Major

Lieutenant Colonel

Colonel

General

The Rebel Yell

Johnny Reb had his own distinctive battle cry which usually was given when he was on the attack. Those who heard the high pitched "Rebel yell" on the battlefields of the Civil War could never forget it. The yell could send shivers up an enemy soldier's spine and, in fact, became an effective weapon for the Southern foot soldier.

Fighting Men and Boys

Although statistics indicate that the bulk of the fighting men of the Confederacy were between the ages of eighteen and thirty-five, many fresh-faced boys and white-haired oldsters found their way into the Southern ranks. Due to shortages in available manpower, youths as young as thirteen, fourteen, or fifteen shouldered muskets. At the other end of the spectrum, a number of men in gray were over sixty years old and at least one was recruited at the age of seventy-three. Near the end of the war Union general Grant observed that the Confederacy was "robbing the cradle and the grave," to maintain its army. Indeed many brave men and boys of all ages fought throughout the war for Southern independence.

The Greatest Snowball Fight of the War—March 22, 1864

During the winter of 1863-64, General Joe Johnston's Army of Tennessee was quartered near Dalton, Georgia. Harsh winter weather set the stage for one of history's greatest snowball fights. It began with a few random tosses between members of General Cheatham's Tennessee Division and Walker's Georgia Division. The fight escalated and soon nearly 5000 troops were engaged. Military ranks were formed and the men maneuvered and charged across the snowy fields. At one point the Tennesseans broke the center of the Georgia line and even captured the colors of the 41st Georgia. Finally, a colonel wisely called a halt to the battle. Many claimed that it was as hard fought an engagement as any waged against the Yankees.

Confederate Rations

Early in the war the Confederate soldiers had plenty to eat and drink since the Southland was primarily an agricultural region. As the war progressed, however, the rampaging armies took their toll of the Southern countryside and Confederate supply lines were often broken. As a result, Johnny Reb often had to depend on his own initiative to keep his stomach filled. He foraged, hunted, and captured food from his well supplied Union foes. Johnny Reb often ate corn bread, sweet potatoes, wild onions, peanuts (goober peas), and corn. Since coffee was in short supply, Johnny Reb often made his hot beverage from peanuts, peas, corn, potatoes and chicory. It was a happy day for Southern soldiers when they captured Yankee rations of coffee or canned goods.

Fifes, Drums, and Bugles

Johnny Reb marched off to war and into battle to the sound of the fife, drum, and bugle. Not only did the drums and bugles provide music in camp and on the march but they were primarily used to convey orders to the soldiers. This was especially important on the battlefield where the commands of the officers were often drowned out by the noise of battle. Drummer boys were often barely in their teens but they had a lot of responsibility and had to learn all the various drum beats which communicated the orders to the soldiers of their units.

Southern Songs

Music was important to the soldiers of the Confederate army and their voices could be heard singing in camp, on the march, and even in the heat of battle. The song "Dixie," of course, was very popular as were other favorites like "The Yellow Rose of Texas" and "Goober Peas." During the battle of Spottsylvania Court House, Virginia, on May 12, 1864, a North Carolina infantryman, Private Tisdale Stepp, helped rally his comrades against a Union attack at the "Mule Shoe" by singing the inspiring Confederate song "The Bonnie Blue Flag." Soon, other soldiers took up the tune and renewed their counterattack.

Religion

Most Confederate soldiers were raised in God-fearing Christian homes and the faith they had in God would help sustain them through the trials of war. In 1863, a great religious revival swept through General Lee's Army of Northern Virginia and from there to the other armies of the Confederacy. Over 100,000 Southern soldiers reaffirmed their faith in God during the revival and Southern camps were often the scene of prayer meetings and hymn singing. Southern preachers urged the men to pray harder, live a true and righteous life, and trust in the Lord.

Cadets of the Virginia Military Institute

One of the most inspiring and dramatic incidents of the Civil War occurred in the Shenandoah Valley of Virginia in the Spring of 1864. As General Franz Sigel led his Union army through the valley, Confederate General John C. Breckinridge called on the teen-age students of the Virginia Military Institute to fill the ranks of his understrength forces. On Sunday, May 15, 1864 264 young cadets gallantly charged a Union battery at the battle of New Market. They captured a Union cannon and several prisoners in hand-to-hand combat. They proudly carried their cherished flag into the battle but,

later, when Union forces burned the school they cut the flag into pieces and gave them to all the cadets to prevent its falling into Yankee hands. Five young cadets were killed at the battle of New Market and five more died later of their wounds. Each year in a special ceremony on May 15, the present-day cadets hold a ceremony to honor those cadets who fell at New Market

Uniforms: all gray.
Flag: white with gold fringe, blue scroll with gold letters.

Confederate Noncommissioned Officers

The men of the Southern forces who wore chevrons on their sleeves were, in many ways, the backbone of the Rebel army. It was the noncommissioned officers who trained the recruits, took care of the soldiers on campaign, and fought beside them in the ranks. Without dedicated NCOs an army would be merely an armed mob and the corporals and sergeants of the Confederate Army set an example of courage and duty that helped keep the army fighting for four long years.

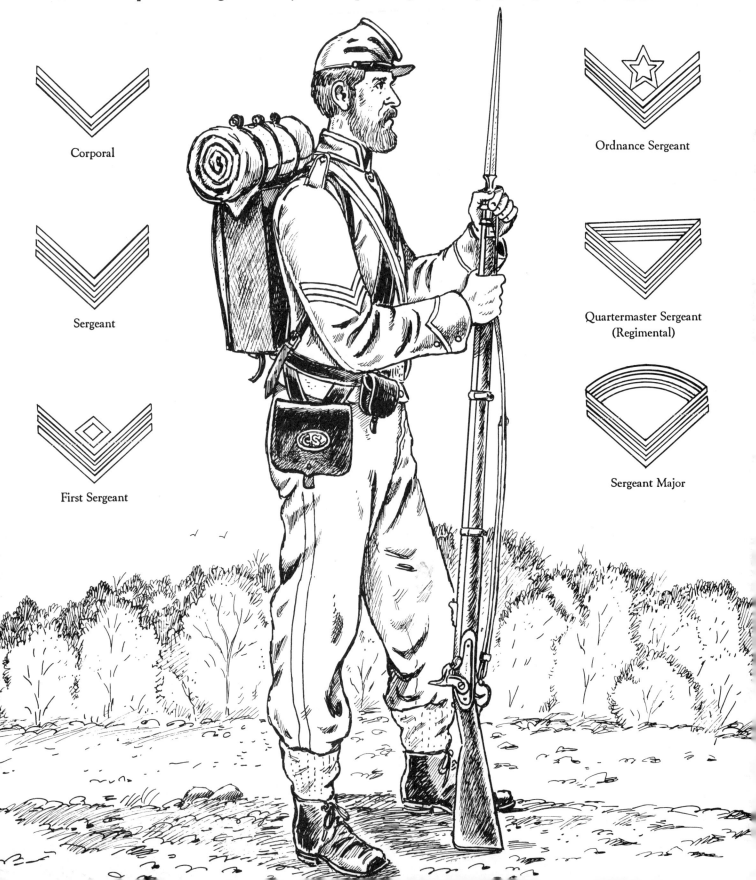

Corporal

Sergeant

First Sergeant

Ordnance Sergeant

Quartermaster Sergeant
(Regimental)

Sergeant Major

Railroads

Railroads played a crucial role in the war for Southern independence. At the beginning of the conflict there was over 8,000 miles of track in the Confederate States, which brought many Confederate soldiers to their first battles. At the battle of First Manassas trains brought reinforcements that turned the tide of battle for the South. Trains also carried supplies and ammunition, and transported the wounded. As the war continued, the Confederate railroad men worked valiantly to keep the trains running in spite of shortages in equipment and the destruction of Southern bridges, tracks, and depots.

The Confederate locomotive Texas was the engine used by the Southern forces to pursue the Union raiders who stole the "General" and drove it north towards Chattanooga in April, 1862.

Confederate troops of General James Longstreet's I Corps detrain at Ringgold, Georgia in September, 1863. They have left General Robert E. Lee's army in northern Virginia to join General Braxton Bragg's army at the battle of Chickamauga. This was the largest single movement by railroad of Confederate troops in the war.

Confederate Sharpshooters

Throughout the war Confederate sharpshooters took their toll of their Union foes earning their respect and fear. Sharpshooters were selected from the crack shots of individual Confederate infantry units. These marksmen were usually exempted from most camp duties but spent their time learning to judge distances and in target practice. The favorite weapon of the Southern sharpshooter was the Whitworth Rifle imported from Manchester, England. The rifle had a twisting hexagonal bore and fired a .45 caliber bullet with great accuracy. For long-range sniping the Whitworth could be fitted with a telescopic sight allowing the marksman to hit targets up to 1500 yards away.

Whitworth bullet

Hexagonal Bore with fitted bullet

Cutaway view of a Whitworth rifle cartridge

WHITWORTH CYLINDRICAL PROJECTILES. 10.- 530 GRAINS

Paper-wrapped cardboard package of Whitworth cartridges

Confederate Medical Department

The Civil War was America's costliest conflict and many Johnny Rebs gave their lives and health to their beloved cause. Over 94,000 were killed in battle while 164,000 died of disease. In addition, over 194,000 were wounded in action. The Confederate Medical Department worked diligently to take care of the sick and wounded soldiers in gray. Although often understaffed and without adequate medical supplies the surgeons, litter-bearers, and civilian volunteers served with dedication and ability. Each Confederate regiment was authorized a surgeon (major), an assistant surgeon (captain), a hospital steward, and two litter-bearers. Hospitals were marked by a red flag.

AMBULANCE CORPS

Hospital knapsack made of wicker covered with black enamelled cloth.

Hat badge worn by enlisted men assigned to duty with the Ambulance Corps. Red band with patch and black stenciled letters.

Confederate Indians

Early in the war the Confederate Government created a Department of Indian Territory to actively recruit Indian soldiers; the troops primarily served in the Oklahoma and adjoining territories. Their Indian war whoops, combined with the Rebel Yell, were certain to impress any foe. The greatest Indian leader of the war was General Stand Watie, who formed the 2nd Cherokee Regiment of Mounted Rifles in 1861. On June 23, 1865, Stand Watie was the last Confederate general to surrender his troops to federal forces.

Most recruits were from the Cherokee, Chickasaw, Choctaw, Seminole, Creek, and Osage tribes.

Mexican Confederates

Mexican-Americans served in the Confederate forces; they were recruited in the Southwest and served in Texan or Louisianan units. The 33rd Texas Cavalry was almost entirely Mexican-American. It was ably commanded by Colonel Santos Benavides, a former Texas Ranger.

The 33rd Texas Cavalry served with distinction along the Rio Grande and in March, 1864 defeated a determined Union force at the Battle of Laredo, Texas.

Texas Colors: Blue; white star and letters; blue numbers; red and white stripes.

Supplies Courtesy of Uncle Sam

In spite of the fact that the Confederate government tried to keep its soldiers supplied with uniforms, equipment, and footwear, Johnny Reb often wore out his gear quicker than his quartermaster could supply it. It was therefore a fortunate day when the Confederates captured a Union supply depot or wagon train. Johnny Reb made good use of captured Union supplies, especially good Yankee shoes, trousers, blankets, and overcoats. Throughout the war Johnny Reb supplemented his supplies with those captured from his well supplied foe.

Confederate Engineers

During the early years of the war the Confederate Engineer Corps consisted only of qualified officers. Enlisted men were detailed from other units when construction work was needed. Late in 1863 two regiments of engineers were finally authorized by Confederate authorities. The First Regiment and two companies of the Second Regiment served in the Army of Northern Virginia. They helped build and defend the fortifications around Petersburg and during the Appomattox campaign built bridges for Lee's army and then destroyed them before the pursuing Yankees could cross them. The other companies of the Second Regiment served in the western theater.

The Confederate Navy

In spite of the fact that the South began the war with few shipyards and little seafaring tradition, the Confederate navy was innovative and courageous. Torpedoes (water mines), ironclad ships, and even a submarine were all used by the Confederates to fight against the superior Union navy. Confederate sailors generally wore gray uniforms and were armed with cutlasses, pistols, and carbines. Near the end of the war naval personnel ashore in the vicinity of Richmond were formed into a battalion and fought in the last battles around the Confederate capital.

Lieutenant

Midshipman

Seamen

The Confederate Marine Corps

The Confederates formed their Marine Corps on March 16, 1861 before the attack on Fort Sumter. Although the Corps was small, it served the Confederacy well, fighting on board ship and on land. Near the end of the war, Confederate marines joined the naval brigade fighting around Richmond. In all, 1,600 officers and men served in the Confederate Marines but there were never more than 600 at any given time. The sergeant and first lieutenant depicted here wear gray uniforms with dark blue trim. The officer also wears a crimson sash and gold shoulder knots. The private in fatigue dress wears a dark blue shirt and hat. His trousers are gray. The men are armed with Enfield rifle muskets and equipped with British-style accoutrements.

Farewell to the Colors

Johnny Reb followed his battle flags gallantly into battle for almost four years and when the war ended and it was time to surrender the beloved banners it created scenes of great emotion. Some units burned their flags while others cut the flags into little pieces and distributed them to members of the unit. When the Army of Northern Virginia surrendered 71 flags on April 12, 1865, at Appomattox Courthouse, many loyal soldiers wept or kissed their tattered emblems of bravery and sacrifice.

Johnny Reb's Return

In the spring of 1865, many weary, ragged, Confederate soldiers, who were loyal to the Confederacy to the bitter end, made their way home to their grateful families. Four years of conflict had thinned the ranks of those who left their homes to defend their Southland in 1861. Over 258,000 men died for the Southern cause and those who returned to their loved ones could be justly proud of their brave service.

Confederate Veterans

Despite the fact that they were defeated, the men who wore the gray could be proud of their gallantry and dedication to the "Lost Cause." As the years passed, the reunited nation, both North and South, came to treasure the heroic legacy of the Civil War and the men who fought it. The United Confederate Veterans became a distinguished organization in the Southern states and the gentlemen "whose beards were as gray as their uniforms" were respected and revered by their countrymen. In time, the ranks of the Confederate veterans thinned, until the nation mourned the passing of the last "Johnny Reb" in 1959.